Dog Star

Written by Janeen Brian

Illustrated by
Ann James

An easy-to-read SOLO
for beginning readers

Scholastic Canada Ltd.
New York Toronto London Auckland Sydney
Mexico City New Delhi Hong Kong

Scholastic Canada Ltd.
175 Hillmount Road, Markham, Ontario, Canada L6C 1Z7
Scholastic Inc.
555 Broadway, New York, NY 10012, USA
Scholastic Australia Pty Limited
PO Box 579, Gosford, NSW 2250, Australia
Scholastic New Zealand Limited
Private Bag 94407, Greenmount, Auckland, New Zealand
Scholastic Ltd.
Villiers House, Clarendon Avenue, Leamington Spa,
Warwickshire CV32 5PR, UK

Text copyright © Janeen Brian 1997.
Illustrations copyright © Ann James 1997.

Cover design by Lyn Mitchell.

First published by Omnibus Books, part of the
SCHOLASTIC GROUP, Sydney, Australia

National Library of Canada Cataloguing in Publication Data
Brian, Janeen
  Dog star
(Solo reading)
ISBN 0-439-98886-1
I. James, Ann   II. Title.   III. Series.
PZ7.B7587Do 2002   j823   2001-900546-6

5 4 3 2 1   Printed and bound in Canada.   1 2 3 4 / 0

To Dyan — J.B.

For Hamish Stephenson and Illlie — A.J.

To Dylan — J.B.

For Hamish Stephenson

Chapter 1

Spud and Jack were friends. They did everything together. If Spud liked something, his tail pointed.

When Spud found a skateboard in the garbage, Jack took it home. He painted silver and red stars on it.

The board looked cool, but the paint was sticky. It needed time to dry.

Chapter 2

Jack took Spud for a walk in the park. Oh, no! The big boys were there, kicking a football.

"What a funny-looking dog,"
cried Bob. "What kind of a dog
is that?"

"That's not a dog. That's a bath
mat!" said Nick. He had a mean
laugh.

Spud growled. He had a mean growl.

"This is my dog. Not a bath mat." Jack put his hand on Spud's neck.

"Come on, Nick," said Bob.
"Forget it. Let's have a game."
Jack and Spud walked home
fast.

Chapter 3

Next day, the paint on the
skateboard was dry.

Jack skated up and down,
up and down the lane.

Spud ran alongside. Jack's hair blew across his face when he went fast. Spud's ears flew back.

Jack did spins and jumps. Spud's
tail pointed. He wanted a turn.
"Not yet, Spud," said Jack.

On Monday, after school, Jack
put his bag in his room. He put his
lunch box on the kitchen table.
Then, with his helmet and his
board, he went out to play.

Spud wanted to skate too.
"Not now," said Jack.

On Tuesday, Spud barked and
jumped in front of Jack.
"Later," said the boy.

Chapter 4

On Wednesday, Spud was sitting
by the skateboard when Jack
came home from school.

"Wait," said Jack. "There's a trick I want to try."

On Thursday, Jack ran inside from the lane.

"Mum, I did a whole turn on my skateboard!" he cried. "A three-sixty!"

"Great," she said. "Can Spud ride yet?"

"Not yet," said Jack.

On Friday he went outside again. He picked the board up.

"Come on, Spud," he said. "It's your turn now."

Chapter 5

Jack put the board down. Then
he put Spud on top of it. The
dog's paws were on stars.

"Stay," said Jack.

Jack put his foot on the back of the board. He pushed it.

Spud's ears flicked up. He began to go fast. He skated all the way to the end of the lane.

Jack ran alongside.

"That's great, Spud," said Jack.
"Faster this time."

Spud stood very still. His tail pointed. His nose pointed. He flew along the lane with his ears out behind him. Jack ran alongside again.

"Good dog. Smart dog," said
Jack. "Now it's my turn." Jack
skated fast up the lane. Spud ran
beside him.

"Your turn again." The dog
skated back down the lane.

Jack ran inside.
"Mum! Spud can skate!"

Chapter 6

On Saturday, Jack made a helmet
for Spud out of an ice-cream tub.
Then he took him to the park that
had the skateboard ramp.

Spud stayed on the board as it swished from side to side on the ramp.

"We should go on television!" Jack said.

Later that afternoon, Jack's mother asked him to get her some flour.

"A two-kilo bag," she said to Jack. "I'm making pizza."

"Yum," he said. "Back in a flash."

Spud and Jack took turns on the board all the way. They went past Mrs. Lock's big yellow dog.

They went past Mr. Pitts' small white cat.

Spud's ears flew out behind him. His tail pointed. His nose pointed.

Chapter 7

At the shop, Jack put Spud's
lead around a pole. He took his
skateboard inside.

"You can't bring that in here," said the shopkeeper.

"I won't ride it," said Jack.

"Outside, please. That's the rule."

Jack went outside.

"Look after our board," he said
to Spud.

It was hard to find the flour.
The shopkeeper had shifted
everything. Jack had to ask.

When he went to pay, there was
a line of people at the checkout.
He had to wait a long time.

Spud stayed on the board. People who went into the shop smiled to see a dog on a skateboard!

Chapter 8

Oh, no! It was the big boys.
Spud's ears stood stiff.
 Bob pointed at Spud.

"Hey, there's that dog we saw in the park," he said. "He's on a skateboard. Do you think he can ride it?"

"Ha!" said Nick. "If he could, he'd be a dog star!" He had a mean laugh.

Spud growled.

"Nice dog," said Nick. He patted Spud. "Give me that board. I'll show you how to skate."

He pushed Spud.

The dog growled again. He had a mean growl.

"Good dog," said Nick.
Spud's lips parted to show
sharp teeth.

Chapter 9

"You won't get that skateboard,"
said Bob. "That dog's smart."
  "Just watch me!" said Nick.

Nick gave Spud a hard push. He grabbed the board.

Spud grabbed him! He sank his teeth into Nick's pants.

"Yow!" Nick cried. "Get him off!"
He dropped the skateboard fast.

"He'll eat me!" cried Nick.

Rip!

"My pants!" he yelled. There was a big hole.

"Nick," said Bob. "Your bottom is showing." He laughed.

Nick put his hands over his bottom and ran.

Chapter 10

Bob sat with Spud. "Are you
OK, dog?"
    Jack came out.

"He's smart, your dog," said Bob.
"Yes," said Jack. "He can skate."
Oh, no! This was one of those
big boys. "Is your friend here?"
Jack asked.

"Nick had to go," said Bob.
"He won't be back. He has some
. . . sewing to do."

Sewing? Jack didn't ask why.
And Bob didn't say.

Bob just said, "Can I watch your dog skate?"

"OK," said Jack.

Spud's tail pointed. His nose pointed. His ears flew out behind.

He was a dog star.

Janeen Brian

I didn't have a dog of my own until I was grown up. Now I have a lovely dog called Nell. She likes to stand at the window and watch the children ride their skateboards. They ride along the lane by my house. That's what gave me the idea to write about a dog on a skateboard.

I enjoy the writing, and I am always thinking of new story ideas. I also love reading and walking along the beach. I get some of my best ideas when I'm out walking.

Ann James

I love drawing animals, especially cats and dogs (I have four cats and one dog). This story has been great fun because I've made Spud look like my own dog, Oliver. Ollie came from the pound. He's black and white and very bouncy. We've been told that he's a Springer Spaniel cross. He's very springy, but he's not often cross. He's the friendliest dog of all!

I like to draw quickly with a pen dipped in ink. If I use colour I nearly always paint with watercolour. It's see-through, so the lines show up well. This is a black and white book so Ollie looks just like he does in real life — except for his dark pink tongue and the grass stains on his ankles.